THE NARRAGANSETT TRAIL

THE NARRAGANSETT TRAIL

A HORROR STORY

TIM O'LEARY

Copyright © 2023 Tim O'Leary.

All rights reserved. No part of this book may be reproduced, stored, or transmitted by any means—whether auditory, graphic, mechanical, or electronic—without written permission of both publisher and author, except in the case of brief excerpts used in critical articles and reviews. Unauthorized reproduction of any part of this work is illegal and is punishable by law.

ISBN: 979-8-89031-546-5 (sc)
ISBN: 979-8-89031-547-2 (hc)
ISBN: 979-8-89031-548-9 (e)

Because of the dynamic nature of the Internet, any web addresses or links contained in this book may have changed since publication and may no longer be valid. The views expressed in this work are solely those of the author and do not necessarily reflect the views of the publisher, and the publisher hereby disclaims any responsibility for them.

One Galleria Blvd., Suite 1900, Metairie, LA 70001
(504) 702-6708
1-888-421-2397

ALSO BY TIM O'LEARY

The Portal

The Entity

The Entity's Child

The Entity's Chosen

Tim O'Hara: His Athletic Life and Times

The Dimensional Gateway

Nowhere to Run: A Story of Maternal Abuse and Recovery

Editorial Assistance to Author Shelley O'Leary

Crying Within

Editorial Assistance to Author Duane Coffill

The Eyes Within

To my Son-in-Law, Author Duane Coffill
President, Horror Writers of Maine

*For his enthusiasm for writing and
the insistence that I take a chance at horror.*

To my Wife, Lynn

*For her eagerness to edit, critique
and encourage me daily. A Shawn
Crawford Fan.*

*To my Daughter Author Shelley O'Leary
For all the support throughout this process.*

*May you all continue to inspire so that stories
may come alive.*

Acknowledgements

I wish to thank my Son-in-Law, Author Duane Coffill, for his encouragement for me to take a chance at writing horror. The days spent at Book Fairs and Borders were especially productive. His camaraderie and positive attitude were infectious. Thanks, Duane, for all your assistance and willingness to share your professional insight.

To my Wife and Daughter, Lynn and Shelley respectively: you both have constantly urged me on to continue to write as a source of entertainment. For you both, you have always ignited my passion to create in story form from my imagination ever engaging. Thank you both for always being there for me.

CONTENTS

Forward xiii

Cast of Characters xv

Present Day 1

Gorham Township, March 1744 11

Present Day 23

Gorham Village 51

257 Main Street, Gorham, Maine 55

About the Author 69

FORWARD

The characters chosen for this writing endeavor are mostly taken from my previous works on time travel using advanced military aircraft. 'The Boss' referred to herein represents 'The Entity' from completed works. Also, fondly referred to by Shawn as 'His Blueness', HE is the One who has directed Shawn Crawford to take on missions that have resulted in saving famous personalities assassinated through time. His travels through, both backward and forward in time via The Portal, a Dimensional Gateway, has given me freedom.

I have mixed historical fact with a fictional account in this book to describe one aspect of Good versus Evil. The locations mentioned in The Narragansett Trail do exist today. The Trail is a common exercise path for many to enjoy on any given day. Lynn and I have walked that course many times during the Maine warm weather months. And we do often see a woman walking her dog from time to time. Not to worry in that we've never encountered an elderly woman with a long silver streak of hair running down the left side of her face!

The Character Samuel Bryant did exist during the mid-18th Century in the Gorham Township. Much of this story is based upon the actual Settler-Indian relationships and events that occurred around the time of the French and Indian War.

I truly hope that you will find this to be an enjoyable reading sojourn. My goal is to bring you into the book as events occur so that you may live and see what my Characters experience. Thank you for taking the chance to read this short story.

Enjoy the Moment!

CAST OF CHARACTERS

SAMUEL BRYANT: One of the earliest 18th Century Settlers in the Gorham Township. Became an Instrument of The Entity after narrowly escaping death at the hands of Indians and The Evil One.

SHAWN CRAWFORD: Time Traveler. Works for his Boss 'The Entity'. Intercepts and prohibits the attempted death of Bryant by those who embrace Evil.

DR. MARTIN WESOLOWSKI: 'Marty' - A Physician, DO, and a People's Doctor. Works at the Maine

Medical Center in Portland, Maine. A Subordinate to 'The Entity' and shares the Power to fight and eliminate Evil.

EMILY ROSS: A precocious eleven-year-old living in Gorham with her parents. Was chosen to be an Instrument of The Entity during the early days of on-going settlement in the Gorham Township. A fierce Believer and Advocate in all that is Good.

MIRIAM SULLIVAN: An Instrument of Evil. Resident in the Gorham Township. Often seen walking her dog along the Narragansett Trail today.

KENNETH CURTIS: Mayor of the Town of Gorham. Very popular with the local clientele in Town. A Shape-Shifter. Full head of grey hair.

POLICE OFFICERS: Duane Coffill and Shelley O'Leary – Initial Investigators regarding the attempted death of Samuel Bryant during the present-day time.

SARAH: A Registered Nurse working at the Maine Medical Center.

TIMOTHY and LYNN O'LEARY: Owners of the final showdown property at 257 Main Street in Gorham. Both Instruments of The Entity, although neither ironically and somewhat humorously, do not recognize one another's role in service to the Good. Tim and Lynn both have no knowledge of each other serving The Entity as need dictates by The Boss. Known by both Shawn Crawford and Doctor Martin Wesolowski, the O'Leary's play a significant role in assuring Good vanquishes Evil.

THE ENTITY, a.k.a,, THE BOSS: A surreal and ethereal light blue Being who orchestrates his Subordinates to combat Evil. Is the Principal Source for all missions conducted by those in His favor?

PRESENT DAY

A branch cracked behind him on the Narragansett Trail. The runner trotted to a stop and turned quickly, and apprehensively. Nothing. The moonlight glistened on the small pool of water in the shallow gully to his left. The attack came swiftly from his right side. He was thrown to the ground while landing hard on his left shoulder by the water's edge. His breath escaped him. Hot foul air engulfed the runner's face as a huge hand, or paw-like appendage, slapped the side of his head violently to the side. The runner saw a mouth full of ragged teeth driving downward onto his exposed neck. The violent pinch and further thrust of the forceful being's jaw radiated excruciating pain throughout his conscious being. The man was rapidly moved from side to side while locked in the beast's razor-sharp teeth. With the runner's eyes fully opened in shock, he saw the full moon above begin to fade, slowly, then rapidly, to nothing.

Seconds later, a spirit-like awareness of the runner's body lying prone on the damp trail appeared below him. He saw his body below twitching from failing nerve endings yet put to rest. His attacker, a beast of a man, or animal, sat sniffing at what it had horrifically broken. The beast, midnight black in color, continued to gaze upon the body that had been ripped apart above the shoulders. Blood no longer pumped from the victim's heart to the neck. Arteries were torn viciously from the torso creating an outlet for the blood that had pooled onto the cool leaves and darkened soil. The beast felt nothing, but a rising curiosity.

A soft swishing sound approached from the other side of the nearby water pool. Both the beast and the runner's ethereal spirit, looking down below, turned quickly to seek its source. There, a movement from a copse of trees nearby. Just beyond the moonlit water. No more than five yards away now. Moving ever so slowly, and deliberately, toward the beast as though a purpose propelled it onward. A mist the color of pale blue approached the huge four-legged animal.

The beast howled in protest at the incursion. It then began to cower as the light blue mist appeared to grow in substance ever so slowly. The bluish, now almost fog-like, mist grew quickly in height and depth, almost with a purpose. The vapor moved forward and soon enveloped the beast completely. An immediate shriek of insufferable pain came from within. Then, nothing.

The light blue mist then rose from the beast's contorted, lifeless body. The runner's spirit hovered above, both in amazement and fear of what was to come. The bluish opaque substance moved slowly upward and surrounded the runner. Now, total silence.

From within, the runner's spirit experienced a sense of overwhelming relief, absent of fear. An invisible touch caressed his face. The feeling was like no other, one that a lover might render to show undying affection. His consciousness faded.

When the runner's sense of being returned, he was lying on his back. The mist was nowhere to be seen. The moon shone brightly above. He was alone. No sign of his attacker. And he was "whole" again. And then suddenly, the darkness enveloped him.

The shrouded figure, having witnessed everything that had transpired, stood hidden behind a large fir tree at the trail's edge. His eyes were those of fire. His face showed intense anger. After a few moments, his body relaxed. A smile soon creased his face. He/it started a slow and deliberate walk, more like a shuffle, toward the unconscious figure. Closer now. A look to the inert beast pre-occupied the figure for several minutes. "Rest in Hell, my friend." he whispered hoarsely toward the dead carcass.

He turned toward the unconscious man lying on the Trail. The inner fury he felt toward the loss of the animal soon resided. His black coarse staff lifted and rested on the chest of the individual barely breathing before him. He slowly dropped to his left knee as the staff was moved aside slowly and deliberately to his left and struck loudly just above the body in front of him. The air turned tepid. A quiet laugh escaped him as his eyes turned fiery red. The smile that could only be described as pure evil returned.

As he bent very slowly toward the body with his head bowing toward the exposed neck of the victim, a shot rang out. It was more like a 'thud' sound rather than a usual sharp retort from a gun or rifle that's fired, such as when a weapon was used with a silencer attached to the end of a gun barrel. Then another 'spit' of a shot, and another, and a fourth, each hitting the black clothed figure in a precise circle around the heart.

The staff was flung aside and the body jerked backward each time he was hit. His feet fell out from beneath him after the final silenced shot and his back slammed heavily onto the middle of the Trail. He remarkably rose quickly to his feet and searched the woods for his assailant. Not seeing anyone, he turned around, grabbed his ebony staff, and rapidly moved off the Trail and into the bushes. From where he disappeared, a dark reddish mist began to rise and a mournful howl echoed harshly about the woods. And then, nothing. Pure silence.

A man emerged on the opposite side no more than 30 meters from the still unconscious runner. The approaching shape that showed itself appeared to radiate a bluish color from head to toe. No, that was inaccurate. The color was more of a bluish lavender hue, bright but not overly so. The individual was dressed in what appeared to be navy blue garb, a one-piece outfit very like what military aviators wore when piloting their supersonic aircraft. He stepped toward the body lying unconscious on the ground while cradling a strange looking rifle in his arms.

When he reached the prone body on the Trail, he looked quickly around him to assure that he was alone and free from danger. He bent over the man and reached out with his right arm to touch the runner's face. He did so with a sense of urgency. An ever so slight smile creased his lips. He rose, looked about, and took one final look at the unmoving runner.

"Be well, Samuel. Be well, my friend," he whispered.

He turned toward the clearing where the football field was located, stopped, and pointed a finger in the direction of where a game was being played. It wasn't the sporting event that was being played on a nearby football field that he pointing to, but rather to the presence of a young girl standing serenely by a tree. After he nodded once and smiled, he said in a soft voice, "Hello, Emily". The gesture was more of recognizing her and knowing that she would be there watching the entire bloody event on the Trail. The girl remained passive and still. The Stranger clad in navy blue attire then moved deliberately off the Trail and into the woods.

A little girl dressed in a white jeans-like contemporary outfit had indeed witnessed the entire gruesome attack that occurred on the Trail. Earlier, Emily had accompanied her parents to watch the Gorham Junior Varsity 'Grizzlies' play their game against Westbrook High School's Freshman Team. While her parents were screaming, and cheering their Gorham Team on, she had unobtrusively wandered over to the nearby wood line. Almost with a purpose in mind. She entered the brush interspersed among the trees and stood very still. She had gone unnoticed by the shrouded figure. The beast had never acquired her scent during the attack.

Emily Ross looked around and approached the unconscious runner. She bent at the waist and reached out and brushed her hand against the runner's left arm at the top of the limb. Her touch would have been soothing had Bryant been conscious enough to feel it. She held her position for what seemed to be a very long time. She then stood straight up and began etching out with her foot a curious symbol around the inert man in the loose dirt.

When she was done, Emily turned and walked back to the football field.

GORHAM TOWNSHIP, MARCH 1744

Samuel Bryant was working tirelessly in his field in the early morning of a beautiful March day. The soil was fertile and promised to yield a good crop later in the year. Bryant and his family were one of four families living outside the small fort a short distance away. The structure offered sanctuary and protection to the Gorham Township families since the Indian uprising in the local area.

There existed bad blood between the Indians who roamed the land throughout the Township. The French and Indian War was a pivotal turn in the dark relations existing between the two groups. As the English were not to be trusted, so it was that the Indians felt a strong animosity toward the white settlers. Bryant was certain that there would be no problems between himself and the neighboring tribe today. His musket was located several yards away and leaning against an old tree stump just in case something would happen. He continued to labor while whistling an old tune his mother years before had sung to him nightly.

Across the clearing and standing hidden within the tree line, a figure of a man stood watching Bryant. He was clad in black clothing with a hood that hid his head. His eyes were dark red and sinister. His gnarled hand held a wooden shaft made of black wood, the color of ebony. He continued his gaze in the direction of Bryant. A few moments passed and he raised his staff and pounded it firmly into the ground before him.

Out of the opposite side of the field in the tree line, two Indians emerged with tomahawks. They were positioned exactly between Bryant and the farmer's log cabin. They were moving toward him at a fast trot while shrieking in a warlike manner. With no time to reach his musket and seeing the danger fast approaching, Bryant dropped his hoe and began running in the opposite direction to the fort to seek shelter from the menacing Indians. The tribesmen knew he would run to the fort when he could not retreat to his cabin.

Bryant scaled a short make shift fence and started up the trail to the fort. He ran as fast as he could. Although Samuel was a huge man of considerable girth, he knew he could not stand a chance against the Indians and their weapons. He got 20 yards beyond the the barrier when two more Indians appeared to his immediate front, they tackled Bryant and tried to force him to the ground.

Samuel was about to dispatch one of his attackers with his bare hands when the second Indian caught Bryant from behind and tomahawked the settler on the back of the head with the weapon's blade facing away. Bryant had moved his head at the last second before the weapon struck his skull. The intense blow drove Bryant to the ground where he lay semi-conscious and moaning.

Two shots rang out from where Samuel had been working in his field. They were fired in rapid succession. The two Indians who had "brushed" Bryant out were rushing forward to join their Tribesmen to share in the victory of a white settler kill. Both fell forward and lay still. A gaping bullet hole dotted the middle of the back of one of the charging Indians. Just as his Tribesman fell forward face down into the Trail's soft surface, the second Indian running alongside tripped over a hidden vine running length wise and just high enough over the ground to catch the leading edge of his moccasin. He immediately went face first onto the hard-packed Trail and hit his head against solid rock lying on the pathway. The action was violent enough to render the Indian unconscious, but still alive. The Shooter's second shot had missed.

The Indian brave's name was Wounded Knee. Thought to have been dead, he was unconscious for a couple of hours before being found by fellow Tribesmen. He was taken to safety where his head wound healed within a matter of hours.

A short distance away, one of the Indians who had brought the white settler down to the ground had taken his sharp knife from his sheath and was kneeling over Samuel. When the Indian heard the two shots in the direction from where Bryant had been working in the field, he looked up apprehensively. Another shot rang out and the back of the scalping Indian's head blew out the back of his skull.

The remaining of the four Indians was dispatched within a matter of seconds in the same manner as his fellow attacker. His chest exploded inwardly when the rifle round entered and severed his backbone as he was pushed backward by the force of the bullet. He fell backward to the ground and lay still, his eyes staring widely at the clear blue sky.

Samuel's body jerked as he moaned loudly while attempting to get up off the ground. His body swayed forward as he tried to get up. He shook his head slowly and yelped out in pain. Bryant then felt strong pressure on his upper right arm as he slowly rose to his feet having found purchase with the ground.

Samuel's eyes still dazed, he tried to focus on the form before him. Finally, some of his double vision dissipated and he made out a young-looking man dressed in navy blue clothing from head to foot. It was a whole one-piece garb with a strange metal fastener to keep both halves together in the front. The stranger steadied Samuel as the latter leaned to the left.

"Are you alright, Sir?" the man asked. Bryant grabbed the back of his head and came away with a smear of blood. He mumbled something about gratitude for the stranger's saving his life. Bryant looked over at the two dead Indians and then to the rifleman.

"Yes, yes, I believe so. That was you who took down these Indians, was it not?"

"I was just fortunate to be in the area when I heard a commotion created by the four Indians wishing to do you harm."

Samuel eyed the man curiously and glanced at his weapon he now cradled in his arms. Bryant had fired muskets a thousand times, but this was no musket he had ever seen before. The rifle had a short barrel and a curious shoulder stock. It was made from some curious gray metal. Hanging out of the underside of the weapon was a lead canister-like protrusion. His Rescuer was obviously no stranger around weapons.

"I want to thank you for saving my life, Sir." Bryant took another moment and studied the man more closely. "I don't believe we've properly met, Mr.?"

His rescuer's eyes shined light blue and appeared to mist briefly before he smiled. He looked Samuel over from head to toe before answering the obvious question for introductions to occur.

"Names are unimportant, Mr. Bryant. Again, I was just glad to have helped. I recommend that you continue along this trail to the Fort. You should be safe enough to gain its access now. You are certain that you are going to be OK, Samuel?" he asked while patting him on the upper arm. Samuel felt the slightest of a pin prick, then thought nothing of it.

Bryant nodded in the affirmative and watched as the stranger turned and began walking along the trail in the opposite direction and across the barrier. As he watched him disappear around the bend in the Narragansett Trail, Samuel witnessed a faint but bluish hue surrounding the figure. And, then the stranger was gone. Very curious, Samuel Bryant thought.

Bryant turned and looked at his dead attackers. As he raised his eyes, he sensed another presence nearby. It gave him chills. It was then that he saw a figure clothed in black and standing beside a tree some 15 meters to his left front, but more off to the side. The being simply stood there and watched

Samuel intently. Bryant noted that the eyes were a bright deep red. He/it carried a long wooden staff in his chalky, white right hand that was gnarled at the joints. Samuel finally began to move after what seemed like a very long moment. He walked briskly down the trail leading to the safety of the Fort.

The cloaked figure stood watching as if waiting for something to happen. It looked downward toward his left foot at the huge four-legged creature lying and growling softly beside him. Its jaws were massive and it was jet black in color, the hue of the being's staff.

"This is not the time," he whispered hoarsely. "Not the time."

From behind, he heard the hiss of a voice, "Why not now?! When will there ever be a time with you?"

The being turned quickly and addressed the woman cowering before him. She was dressed in rags, not very tall, large brown eyes, and dark black hair with a silver streak running down the left side of her head. The being's tone rose in such an evil manner that filled her with unmistakable fear. "Do not question me, woman!" His eyes fiery red began to subdue as he stepped toward the figure before him. He slammed his staff into the ground with such power that the woman fell backward, trembling with fear.

"Rise, Miriam. And leave me quickly before I set the hound upon YOU!!"

She started to get up but caught one of the backs of her feet on a vine sticking up out of the ground. The woman turned on all fours, stumbled forward, and ran shrieking into the wooded area The being stared after her departure and nodded slowly. The beast below him growled ominously.

"She will one day be very important to me. She will, indeed, my pet."

Bryant reached the clearing's edge leading up to the wooden fort. Everything turned hazy to him and he fell to the ground in shock. An eleven-year old girl picking flowers by the fort's wall saw Samuel drop to the ground. She immediately yelled for help and unconsciously started running toward the inert man. A sentry called out sharply, "Emily, wait!!"

A shout was heard within the fort and three rugged settlers exited through the front gates and ran down the Trail after the girl. They carried their muskets in one arm and soon reached Emily standing over Samuel. Bryant had gained conscious for just a moment while the girl was leaning over him. He grabbed the girl unexpectedly high on her left arm. She felt the briefest of pain. She pulled back hurriedly.

"Emily, get back to the fort right now!" one of the men shouted. "Thomas, take her up to the fort and sound the alarm." the leader of the small group ordered as he looked for any sign of impending danger from the Trail.

Both remaining men lifted Bryant on either side and dragged him up and into the wooden structure. The gates were quickly shut and barred from the inside after the leader of the group and Emily were secured within the walls. A woman came running over and saw the gash on the rear side of Bryant's head. She immediately crossed the courtyard and went into one of the small rooms. She came out with water and bandages a few moments later.

They took Samuel's leather shirt off and checked for any other wounds. The woman noticed something very peculiar. There was a small but easily identifiable pale bluish tinge, more like a symmetrical mark, on Bryant's upper left arm. She paid no further attention to it and began to cleanse the head wound.

As she was administering to Samuel, they heard the sound. It was like no other. It was banshee-like and it sent chills down the spine of all who heard it from within. More men appeared and climbed the steps to the landing at the top of the wall. They saw nothing in the wooded area that cradled the Trail.

Sentries would be doubled that evening.

PRESENT DAY

The Narragansett Trail was a mile and one-quarter loop that began and ended halfway up Chick Street from the Gorham Public Safety building. The newly-constructed structure housed the local law enforcement agency, as well as the attached Gorham Fire and Rescue Unit. The entire Trail/pathway was considered safe for those who walked or trotted the Trail distance. "Gorhamites", especially those enjoying their retired and senior years, frequented the trail daily to get in their exercise for the day. The Author and his lovely Wife of 38 years, Lynn, frequented the use of the Trail four days a week during the warm weather months. At a brisk walk, it took some 17-20 minutes to complete the circuit depending upon the whim of the trail user's pace. It was well traveled during the late Spring to early Fall months. As a matter of fact, the Gorham High School Track Teams utilized the Trail to conduct their Class A interscholastic competition when school was in session.

An elderly woman living in an adjoining housing development had been walking her dog along the Trail at 6:00 AM. She came across a young man lying inert in the middle of the Trail and immediately pulled out her cell phone and dialed 911. Within five minutes of the completed call, the Gorham Rescue Unit had arrived and paramedics immediately began attending to the unconscious individual. The stretcher carrying the runner's body was lifted gently and placed into the rear of the ambulance a short distance away. It was 6:30 in the morning.

The woman smiled as she led her huge black dog away and along the pathway. She continued her regimen of daily exercise until she reached a small clearing off the Narragansett Trail. She walked the few steps to her two-story clapboard home located in one of Gorham's endless home developments. The elderly woman let the dog loose by dropping the leash and it bounded up the stairs to the front door. It turned toward the woman and waited patiently.

The front door then appeared to open inward by itself toward the inside foyer. The immense dog stayed inert until the woman raised her right hand slightly to her waist. The dog turned and, with just enough space to enter, bounded into the house with a low growl. The woman then turned her head 180-degrees without moving her body back to where the Trail joined the clearing. Her head then rotated back to the front steps of the building and she slowly walked up the stairs. Before entering the house, a breath of arid air blew softly in her direction, tossing the single white streak of hair on the left side of her face away from her head. She entered the house. When completely inside, the door appeared to shut by itself. Not a sound was heard at that point. The chirping of the birds ceased almost immediately.

The unconscious victim along the Trail was immediately ferried to the Maine Medical Center in Portland and to the Emergency Room entrance. Vital signs had been relayed to the hospital by the attendant riding in the back via cell phone. When the vehicle stopped at the entrance, medical personnel came out quickly and aided in getting the man into a Trauma Room. One doctor and two nurses rushed into the room.

As the doctor was in the process of examining the inert figure, the man's eyes opened widely as a surge of air was inhaled into his lungs. The man's body jerked once and then he lay still. The eyes shown light blue in color. He attempted to rise from the table, but one of the nurses held him down while telling him that he was alright and safe now. He relaxed.

"Where . . .? It looks like I'm in the hospital," he said. "Why am I here?" he asked.

"Just relax, Sir. My name is Marty Wesolowski. I'm a resident physician here at the Maine Medical Center. You were brought into the Trauma Unit early this morning. It's Thursday morning. Please tell us your name, Sir," Dr. Marty said.

"My name is Samuel Bryant, Doctor", he replied. "What happened to me?"

"Mr. Bryant, please call me 'Marty'. All my patients do. You were found lying unconscious on the Narragansett Trail in Gorham. A woman by the name of Miriam Sullivan was walking her dog on the Trail early this morning and found you. She immediately called 911 and the Gorham Rescue Unit personnel arrived shortly thereafter. Are you in any pain, Mr. Bryant?" Samuel replied in the negative.

"We were not able to identify any next of kin, Sir. Do you have family here in the local area?"

"Ah, no. I'm a widower. This is all very surreal to me. I don't feel any pain anywhere in my body. I, I don't remember anything after entering the Trail last evening. Wait, there was a huge animal that bounded very quickly in front of me on the path."

Bryant then attempted to get up and one of the nurses stopped him. "Ma'am, please take your hand off me," Samuel said in a reassuring smile. "I am alright now. Just a bit disoriented. Let me swing my legs over the edge here and take a couple of deep breaths."

The nurse started to hold him down and was soon assisted by another medical professional. "Mr. Bryant, please lie still until we can make sure you're able to get up on your own," insisted Dr. Marty.

At that moment, two of Gorham's police officers entered the large cubicle. One of the officers who appeared to be in charge looked at Dr. Wesolowski and asked, "May we speak to the gentleman, Marty?" As it was a relatively small Town, familiarity with one another, professional or no professional, was a pleasant aspect appreciated by all in Gorham.

"Duane, please give us a few more minutes with Mr. Bryant," the physician replied.

Both officers then left the room. As quickly as they left, the Mayor of Gorham, the Honorable Kenneth Curtis, entered with a big smile. Before he could say anything, Dr. Wesolowski politely and sternly asked to him to wait outside. Mayor Curtis frowned slightly, turned on his heel, and proceeded to the Waiting Room where he met the two Gorham Police Officers. No one spoke as they all took chairs across the room.

Mr. Curtis, a head of hair completely silver in color, had been elected Mayor for the past eight elections in a Town that welcomed anyone with a big heart and the willingness to dedicate his life toward the enhancement of good relationships. In other words, he was the People's Mayor.

Of course, the position of Mayor in the Gorham Township was but a part time responsibility for him. Curtis owned half of Gorham's property that had been handed down from generation to generation.

He owned and operated the Gorham Savings Bank located in the middle of Town and across Main Street from the Town's only Funeral Home. He also owned and operated the Home, mostly in the evenings.

When the Medical Team had finished examining Samuel, Dr. Wesolowski came into the Waiting Room and addressed everyone.

"Mr. Mayor, please allow the law enforcement officials to go in first and question Mr. Bryant alone. When they are finished, you may go in. Officers, Mayor, I am giving you not more than 5 minutes for questioning. Mr. Bryant is to be scheduled for an MRI and blood work. I want him to remain here overnight for observation. If everything looks good in the morning, I will discharge him from the hospital. However long you folks need now to talk to him, it's up to you. But, I will be coming back here in 5 minutes and end all conversations. Is this understood by everyone?"

All three individuals nodded in the affirmation. Dr. Wesolowski then left the Waiting Room and began talking to the attending RN just outside. One of the Gorham Police Officers then asked Mr. Curtis to wait patiently while they initiated their investigation. Curtis began to object, thought better of it, and nodded with a frown. The Officers returned to the Trauma Room.

"Mr. Bryant, my name is Officer Coffill and this is Officer O'Leary," he nodded to his woman counterpart. "We won't be long, but we do have to ask you a few questions, if you are up to it." Samuel nodded that it was OK.

"Please tell us what you remember from last night."

Bryant then recounted as best he could the events of the previous evening. In effect, all he could bring back to memory was the attack by a huge beast as he had begun to jog along the Narragansett Trail. There had been a Gorham Junior Varsity football game on the field apart from the Trail and very near the Gorham Safety Building. Fans of the Gorham Team were shouting relating to a play that was happening at the time of the attack. And then he mentioned that he saw his body from above lying bleeding on the Trail below. It was a surreal experience he said. And then, he remembered waking up here in the hospital.

"We found evidence of an animal carcass not far from where the Rescue Unit personnel found you. It looked as though it had been incinerated. It had the shape of a dog, but this thing was massive! Any memory of what that animal was that may have attacked you, Mr. Bryant?" asked Officer O'Leary.

"No, like I said, after seeing my body lying below, everything kind of blacked out. What really happened, do you know?" he asked.

Coffill then replied that his Team were still combing the Trail area for clues. "We'll be back later for some more questions after we've reviewed the site, Mr. Bryant. In the meantime, get some rest. Thanks for the information. We'll talk later."

When the Officers had left, Mayor Curtis rushed into the room. "Mr. Bryant, how are you feeling," he asked with a sincere tone of concern. "I learned of this horrible situation this morning over the police scanner. I briefly overheard something about a "beast" attacking you on the Trail. Is, that right?"

Samuel then recounted everything he had told the police. There was nothing more that he could add after the Mayor continued to probe for more information. Curtis then wished him well and left the room hurriedly. Bryant thought that all of what just happened with the Mayor was more than a bit unusual.

Samuel was kept overnight for observation in a semi-private room. Numerous tests during the day following his admitting had been administered with negative results showing. Still, Doctor Wesolowski insisted that Bryant remain overnight for observation purposes. It was more private than anything else for patients staying at the Maine Medical Center this evening were very few on the Ward. Not long after he got to his room, he fell into a deep sleep. At 2:30 AM he awoke with a start. He looked around and then was startled by a presence sitting in a chair by his bedside. He could tell it was a man by the Burberry cologne odor to him.

Bryant started to go for the call button by his pillow when the man said, "Hello, Samuel, no need to call the nurse on duty. I mean you no harm. I'm pleased to see that you have been well taken care of since I left you last evening." His eyes glinted a pale blue. His face was serene and Samuel immediately began to feel at ease.

Samuel squinted and, when his eyes adjusted, he had no memory of ever seeing this person before. As to his reference to last night, he remembered only being attacked by a horrific creature while jogging along the Trail not far from the roadway. He was now stunned at the sight of anyone sitting in his room in the middle of the night. The Stranger was wearing a one-piece dark uniform.

A moment later, Dr. Wesolowski came into the room. What in the world is Marty doing here at close to three in the morning? The doctor looked over at the individual sitting in the room and showed no surprise at all.

"Shawn, it's good to see you again, my Friend. It has been a while since we last saw one another, hasn't it?" Marty said with a small and curious smile that Bryant could just barely make out in the dim light from the corridor.

"Hello, Marty. Yes, it's been nearly a year and a half since we had an 'episode'. I'm just glad I was in the area last night when Samuel here was attacked by that She-Wolf."

Marty looked over at Bryant and nodded. "I'm glad you were. It appears that it's starting all over again."

Marty closed the door behind him and the room lit up in a soft blue light that permeated the room. It appeared to be coming from both the stranger and the doctor. *What in the world is going on here?* Marty attempted to make sense of what was occurring before him. *And, if I do make sense of this*, he said to himself, do I really want to be a part of it? I feel like I'm "drowning" in confusion!

Shawn looked at Marty for a long moment then turned to look at Samuel. He could only imagine what was going through Bryant's mind now. A She-What?!? He chuckled to himself and then spoke to Dr. Wesolowski.

"I think it may be the right time to "plug" Samuel into what is going here." He sat forward in his chair while turning fully in Bryant's direction. Shawn's pale blue eyes appeared to grow "deeper in hue". He glanced quickly at Marty and then back to Samuel.

"Do you have any idea who your descendants are, Samuel? I mean, not just your immediate biological heritage, but farther back than then. Have you ever done an ancestry study of your family background?"

"Well, no, I haven't. Why is that important to me now?" he asked while casting a side long glance at Marty.

"Let me take you on a little history ride that you may just find fascinating, and unbelievable. Your great, great grandfather was Samuel Bryant. He was one of the Founding Fathers of the Gorham Township. With the French and Indian War occurring in the mid-18th century, this area, barely settled by white people, sustained much bloodshed at the hands of warring Indian Tribes who had taken sides with the French. As the small number of inhabitants of the Town were essentially of English descent, and the War was against the British, the native Indians began to distrust the white settlers because of their affiliation and heritage with the British Isles. They had taken sides with the French.

"Your ancestor was one of four settler families that lived outside a fort constructed on the northern side of the Town. Today, Fort Hill that overlooks the countryside to the West was the site of that fort where settlers sought shelter against the numerous Indian raids that occurred weekly in the area.

"To shorten this up a bit, your great, great grandfather's name was Samuel Bryant." Shawn paused and let all that sink in before continuing.

Before being able, the hospital room window on the fourth floor imploded. Both Shawn and Marty yelled at Samuel, "Get down!!"

An eerie moment passed with a very little wind passing through the ruptured casing. A fast-moving form passed by the hospital window. Shawn immediately went over to the bed where Samuel lay bleeding from cuts attributed to shard glasses whirled in his direction. Marty, at the same time, went over to Bryant and speedily checked him over for serious injury. He found none. By then, Shawn had gone over to the window area and looked around, below and above, for any sign of whatever had passed so swiftly by. He saw nothing and quickly went over to Marty who was helping Samuel out of his bed.

"Marty let's get him to a secure location well within the outside windows of the hospital," Shawn insisted.

"I know where we can take him immediately. Samuel, can you walk alright?"

Bryant, with blood dripping from a forehead gash and from a severely lacerated left arm, said that he could. He took two steps and began to fall forward. Marty on the right and Shawn on the left, protecting his injured limb, walked slowly out of the room and to the elevator. By this time, the RN on duty had just reached the patient room doorway. She looked incredulously at Bryant and the blood, Dr. Wesolowski, and the stranger in navy blue garb. Her mouth was wide open.

"Sarah, get the elevator button, will you?" Marty asked with clear calm.

"Of, of course, Marty! What in the hell happened?" she yelled. She pushed the Down Button on the elevator. Sarah then peaked into the room and saw what once was a window along with pieces of glass everywhere in the room. Blood stained the bed sheets. Sarah then shrieked and shrunk back from the open door and backed into the opposing wall.

"Sarah, what is it?" asked Marty as Shawn immediately went to the room's opened door. The latter quickly pulled out a semi-automatic pistol and began firing in the direction of the broken window. Shell casings dropped hotly to the floor.

"Marty, let's get out of here!" he yelled.

The elevator door opened at the same moment. Both men assisted Bryant into the elevator. Sarah went in last and immediately hit the Close Button. The elevator immediately began a descent to the bottom floor.

"Sarah," Marty said calmly, "I want you to dial 911 on your cell phone right now. Tell the dispatcher to send the police and fire department over to the building immediately."

"But, but there is no fire, Marty!"

As if on cue, an explosion rocked the building and shook the elevator on its downward flight. They could not see it for the elevator ceiling but a perfectly round hole with pieces of building concrete with jagged sharp edges pointing inward from the fourth floor smoldered above them. Fortunately, the elevator continued to the lower floor as the explosion miraculously missed the taught cables that held firmly. The electricity never faltered. "There is now!" the doctor replied.

Portland, Maine's Police, Fire and Rescue Units were known for their speedy response to crises in their long history of fighting crime, putting out fires, and administering immediate and quality first aid to victims. Located just down Congress Street, the main artery running east and west through downtown Portland, Units were there in just a matter of moments.

The Police response was immediate. Cruisers immediately cordoned off streets from Park Avenue to the Western Promenade, Spring Street, and those running perpendicular all the way to Outer Congress leading to the hospital complex. Miraculously, medical personnel attending the scene found no one injured in the blast. The Fire Department moved quickly to stem the fire emanating from a localized area on the fourth floor. The entire hospital was still being evacuated as patients on gurneys and those ambulatories were issued warm blankets. The west parking lot began filling with patients and medical staff. In response to the blast, area law enforcement and fire officials responded by providing ancillary support to the local authorities.

No one saw four individuals walking nonchalantly out the rear of the building. They turned up the street a block away, walked 50 meters, turned left, and arrived at Shawn's old Volkswagen Bus. They stopped so that Marty could look at Samuel's lacerations. He took a roll of gauze and a small bottle of betadine from his white coat and administered to the cuts. Sarah, still in shock, assisted as needed.

"Nice wheels," Marty quipped. "Who's got the Turbo tonight?"

"Christine had a mission back in, or I should say, forward in 2074. HE does keep us busy. Christopher is piloting the Sea Avenger. If I know my Son, he's probably doing barrel rolls as soon as the wheels were up! Christine has to look green in the gills by now."

Christine was the lovely golden-haired bride (of many years now) of Shawn Crawford. Christopher was the Child of The Entity who had "adopted" his parents during a mission that Shawn, a Fighter Pilot, had flown while crossing back in time for saving Mahatma Gandhi from assassination, one of many missions given to him by The Entity. It's a long story; you'd have to have read the book, or would have had to have been there.

Sarah, meanwhile, sat in the back with Bryant. Her mouth wide open said, "Who are you two? I thought I knew you, Marty, but everything that has happened this early morning is a bit hard to believe."

Marty turned half-way around in the passenger seat in front and spoke very calmly to the Nurse. His eyes shown a striking glint of pale blue. "Sarah, please be at ease. I will explain as much as I can when we are safely away from the hospital complex."

The Volkswagen turned a corner toward the East End of Portland when it was rocked from above. A crease showed inside as though something very heavy had been dropped on the vehicle. Sarah shrieked!

Another jolt and this time the roof was torn off the chassis. Shawn could barely stay in control of the vehicle. A giant claw reached down inside the back-seat area and lifted Sarah completely out of the still moving vehicle.

"Sarah!!" Marty shouted. Her screams could be heard as she was carried off toward Casco Bay. Then, not a sound, other than a rushing wind through the opening above. Samuel was crouching behind Shawn's seat. He was visibly trembling.

"Samuel, are you alright!" shouted Shawn, knowing all too well that Sarah was gone for good. Marty at the same time reached in back and checked as much of Bryant as possible without slowing down the vehicle.

They soon arrived at the Portland Cathedral near the corner of Cumberland and Franklin Streets. Shawn parked the vehicle, jumped out, and opened the driver's rear door. Marty went up the stairs to the front door of the Church. Not to his surprise, it was locked. He looked intently at the door handle and a sharp and pointed laser of blue surrounded the door. He pushed inward and the huge wooden structure opened inwardly. Shawn assisted Samuel up the stairs and into the Church's foyer. The door closed quietly behind them on its own.

Marty was the first to notice a slim shape sitting in one of the front pews before the altar. He went down the aisle and stopped beside the figure. It was a girl of no more than eleven or twelve. "Hello, Emily," the physician said quietly.

The girl remained staring straight ahead. She slowly turned her head to the left, smiled, and said softly, "Hello, Doctor."

"Please, young lady, I have asked you before to call me 'Marty'. We are not strangers, are we?"

"Of course not, Marty," she replied with a sweet smile. "And, Shawn, it's good to see you again. How are the Children and Christine?" she asked.

"They're all well, thanks for asking. Christine is on another boondoggle. HE certainly keeps us busy, doesn't HE?" Shawn said referring to his Puppet Master, The Entity.

'Yes, HE certainly does that. Hello, Mr. Bryant. It's been quite a while since we've seen one another last. How are his wounds, Marty?" she asked impishly.

"All superficial. He was very lucky. Glass shot inwardly everywhere in that room at the hospital. It appears to be beginning all over again, doesn't it?"

Emily looked pointedly at both men. Her eyes shone brightly with intense blue color. It matched those of both Shawn and Marty. She then directed her gaze at Samuel.

"Does he know what is going on here, Shawn?" she asked while still peering intently at Samuel Bryant.

"I was in the process of filling him in historically when, and after Marty arrived at the room, the window blew inwardly with, shall I say, more than a little bit of purpose." The rest is just our getting out as quickly as possible. We did lose Sarah, the Registered Nurse, on the way over to the Church."

"Yes, Sarah was a good woman in this lifetime. Please know, both of you, that she is being well looked after as we speak. Mr. Bryant, you may find this awkward of my asking, but would mind taking off the 'Johnnie' you are wearing. I'm sorry, Sir, just the top part showing your upper arms and chest."

He looked at both Shawn and Marty who nodded slowly for him to comply. Samuel dropped the 'Johnnie' to his waist. With shoulders exposed, a soft bluish tinge emanated from the top of his left arm. It pulsated very faintly. As Emily reached toward the spot, the color on his arm intensified brightly. Its radiance cast all present in a very soft blue.

Samuel jumped abruptly as Emily touched the spot. She held her hand softly against his arm. Emily's face began to glow, slowly at first, then in intensity. A smile crossed her face as she closed her eyes and started to breathe deeply. Bryant simultaneously relaxed almost transfixed by the touching. He too sensed a calming effect coming over him.

After what seemed like more than several minutes, Emily opened her eyes and directly faced Bryant. Her stare was memorizing. Shawn and Marty waited.

"They are coming for us tonight," she said. "Shawn, you know what to do. Marty, you are to protect Samuel at all cost," she insisted.

Both nodded their heads. Samuel, for a reason known only to Emily, sat in the pew showing calm. He turned his eyes to the other three and then winced with pain. Bryant reached back to the side of his head and his hand came away with a smear of blood. He smiled after a few seconds and looked to Marty.

"I now seem to know what this is all about. Marty, don't be concerned. This is just a reminder of times past and a debt I owe to one that is pure evil."

Emily reached over beside her and handed Samuel a medium-sized gym bag. She instructed him to go into the vestry and change out of the 'Johnnie'.

"These should be your size, Samuel." He went into the side room as directed.

Once Bryant had dressed, they all moved to the front door of the Church. Emily pulled the door to her and a howling shriek filled the air! A bat-like animal pushed the door fully open and began flying about the Church ceiling. Its huge shape rested on one of the statues of the Saints displayed around the Cathedral.

"Looks like our 'friend' is back, Marty," quipped Shawn. "Please, everyone sit quietly in this back pew while I teach our intruder a few manners."

Crawford moved forward down the center aisle as the creature left its perched and dived directly for Shawn. Crawford pulled out his weapon, with silencer affixed to the end of the barrel, and took careful aim. Three 'spits' of the weapon erupted.

The first round hit the right wing at the juncture of where it joined to the immense body. It kept on coming. The second round hit the main body of the flying beast in the mid-section. The final shot found its mark by tearing through the head of this unearthly aberration. No more than three feet separated

Shawn from the diving creature before it dropped immediately to the flooring. Its eyes were still moving slowly as it looked up at Shawn. Crawford put another round in its cranial cavity for good measure.

"Good night, Irene," he said sarcastically.

Marty came over slowly and said to Crawford as they both stood looking down at the dead carcass. "Does Christine know that you are acquainted with this Irene?" he asked sardonically.

Before Crawford could respond with his customary wit, Emily said, "If you Boys are done playing, we do have to go. Not bad shooting, Shawn," she summarized.

They exited the Church and climbed into Crawford's Volkswagen Bus. "Can you get us something new next time?" Marty asked.

'My Friend, there is not going to be a 'next time'," Shawn glibly replied.

They drove off toward the Gorham Township via I-295 and took the Congress Street West Exit.

GORHAM VILLAGE

Mayor Curtis had driven to Miriam Sullivan's two-story house just off the Narragansett Trail for a meeting with her. Very little light shown from the inside. Curtis climbed the few steps and before he could get to the front door, it opened for him just a crack. He entered, but not as a man, but a shape-shifting wolf, gray in color with yellowish-tinted eyes. In the first- floor dining area, on the hardwood floor, sat a hooded figure in the corner of the room. His eyes were deep red. He sat unmoving.

"I am pleased that we are all here. We can get started. Mr. Curtis, you are as late as usual," the dark figure reprimanded.

The Wolf, Mayor Curtis, lay on the floor facing his Accuser, head up, with a forlorn look in his eyes. Its ears were perked up straight above its head as if waiting for punishment to me meted out.

"No need to get dramatic with me, Mr. Mayor. I need you too much to dole out more than this reprimand. Sit. Miriam, bring me the special tall hot tea, as hot as you can make it."

Miriam went over to her kitchen area and, having anticipated the request, had prepared a concoction that one would never find in a recipe book. She poured some into a large tankard and brought it over to him. Mayor 'Wolf' Curtis licked his chops at the smell and sight of the scalding vessel.

The figure rose a bit from the flooring and took in a large measure of the liquid. He put the tankard down between his legs and looked at both Sullivan and Curtis. His appearance began to change. The ebony-colored hood rolled back behind his head. He then rose to his feet. Before them was a youthful-looking man in his mid-20's.

Staring at both figures before him, he said, "I have a mission for both of you this evening. We are going to end this 'competition' between ourselves and The Entity's Guardians. This is what we WILL accomplish this evening. And, do NOT fail me this time! I have a debt to re-pay to one who goes by the name of Crawford!"

Miriam and Curtis sat intently as instructions were given. When concluded, Miriam sported a very wide smile. Curtis' tail was swishing back and forth behind him rapidly. They all left the house and climbed into an unobtrusive 2012 gray Toyota Prius. Curtis, when reaching the door to exit the home had resumed his human shape. He was driving with Miriam sitting in the passenger seat. The 'younger-looking' individual sat in the back without a sound. Curtis put the Prius in drive and they slowly pulled out of the driveway and onto the street.

The air was deathly still.

257 MAIN STREET, GORHAM, MAINE

It was purported to be the first house in the Gorham Township that received electricity. The original foundation was laid circa 1901. The house on that foundation burned to the ground around late Spring 1912 under mysterious circumstances. The Owner at the time was recorded to be a descendant of Samuel Bryant, one of the Township Founders. It was finally restored during late Summer 1912, as indicated by later in the discovered newspaper insulation used in the day and found in the walls. The sales on women's' clothing displayed portrayed an economy of a vastly different era. The dates of sales were annotated in the Fall of 1912.

At its present location, this property was not an obvious dwelling for those traversing Route 25 from the Portland-Westbrook areas to the East and the Town of Standish a short distance to the West. It had gray clapboard shingles and it nestled on busy State Road 25 nearly across the street from the Gorham Public Safety Building. The Owners, Timothy and Lynn O'Leary had purchased the property on July 1, 1979 from the previous Resident, a Mrs. Lynn Joy. She sold the property, it was said, because she firmly believed that 'spirits' roamed the unfinished cellar basement. She tendered a bill of sale for the property at $37,000 to the O'Leary's who bought the small two bedroom second-story home, their first starter and only home purchased in their 38 years of marriage.

It was also said that the home had been initially constructed over an old Indian Burial Ground. Native Indians who were slain by the original founders of the Township were rumored to have been laid to rest without ceremony just under the foundation and concrete cellar flooring. Shelley, the Daughter of the O'Leary's, was said to be 'insightful' and that she had repeatedly mentioned to her Mother that she had seen Spirits moving throughout the entire house on occasion. Even the parents were unable to account for mysterious noises mostly heard in the middle of the night. It was not unusual either during an afternoon to hear a baby cry out where there were no infants present.

To the rear of the home rested an old deserted barn. It was reported that bats were observed flying from the rooftop structure at night. The flooring within was hard dirt packed. A few shelves remained affixed to the side walls. Barn cats roamed freely in and out during the Maine warm weather months. It was dark during the day with very little light filtering through from above. At night, it was pitch black inside.

Mayor Curtis stopped the vehicle on the hill just to the East of the O'Leary home. All three individuals got out. Curtis immediately shape- shifted to the immense gray wolf that he was. He led the way down the hill to the barn. Miriam followed the four-legged beast with the dark clad youthful stranger, carrying his ebony staff, bringing up the rear. They entered the barn and Curtis searched the area inside to insure they were alone. There were lights on in the O'Leary household.

They found their way to the exact middle of the barn and stopped. The stranger's eyes shown fiery red. Miriam was giggling in anticipation of the confrontation yet to come. Curtis laid down in abeyance to his youthful master within touching distance of the black cloak's hem. With eyes now intensely red, the figure pounded his staff forcefully into the ground. Not more than 30 seconds passed when an apparition presented itself to the group's left front. It was an Indian from the 18th century.

"Welcome back, the evil person greeted. Not long now. Not long."

Shawn and his three passengers passed Brackett Road in the Gorham Township on their way to the O'Leary home. Crawford had known Tim O'Leary for years. The latter was also an Instrument of The Entity. His Wife Lynn had never known his identity. They pulled into the driveway at 257 Main Street, stopped the Volkswagen, and got out of the vehicle. Shawn led the way to the side steps leading to the house, followed by Emily, Samuel, and Marty. It was 11:45 PM. Tim was waiting at the door when they entered the closed-in porch that lead into the kitchen. Lynn had retired at 9:30 PM.

"Shawn, it is really great to see you again. Hello, Bones," acknowledging Doctor Marty. Emily passed him into the kitchen with a quick peck to the cheek. Samuel and Marty entered last. The doctor grinned and asked O'Leary if he was still wearing his compression socks daily as prescribed. Tim nodded that he was. There was only one light on and that was in the living room that faced the deserted barn out back.

"Are we all set, Tim?" Shawn asked.

"Yes, Sir, everything is in order. They have arrived at the barn. Something is going on inside as I witnessed a flash of reddish light coming from within and toward the barn's center not more than five minutes ago. How do you want to handle this, Shawn?'

Crawford outlined his plan as all listened intently. Emily's face, as usual, remained calm, though her eyes shone brightly in a steady pale blue. Marty checked Samuel over who insisted that he was OK for now. They were preparing to exit via the cellar bulkhead door when the living room window shattered showering Marty with shards of glass.

"I'm fine!" he yelled. Go, go, go!"

They went down the stairs to the basement. At the far end was the door leading out to the backyard and to the barn some 50 meters away and to the left. First to exit the building was O'Leary who was immediately met by the 'Mayor' of the Gorham Township. The huge and very strong gray wolf knocked Tim off his feet and he landed adjacent to the concrete abutment to the cellar door. Shawn came out next, looked immediately to the struggle to his left, and fired two silenced rounds into the 'Mayor's' torso. The huge gray wolf rolled over and off to O'Leary's left. It was still alive, but breathing heavily. Blood oozed from two wounds.

"Sorry, Timmy. Got to go! This is not your nap time, Brother. Get up and get moving!"

O'Leary did so and veered sharply to the left. Marty still suffering from cut glass, exited and went to the right. Emily calmly walked up the bulkhead stairs and stood facing Miriam, who had stepped out from behind a tree. The latter's silver streak on the left side of her face seemed to glow in the moonlight.

"Hello, Miriam. How long has it been now? A couple of hundred years at least?" Emily sarcastically ventured.

Miriam cackled loudly and lunged for Emily with a short saber-like blade pointed at the latter's heart.

The young girl rotated her body 90-degrees and saw the blade sail by her sternum. Miriam's momentum carried her to Emily's side. The young girl chopped down with her hand on the old woman's arm and contacted a force that produced a blinding bluish hue. The force within that color dropped Miriam to her knees. The Witch looked up and into the pale bluish eyes of the youth.

"I am far from done, girl!"

"Oh yes, you are, Miriam. Go join the hounds in Hell where you belong. Good-bye, old lady." With that, she rose both arms high into the air and came down swiftly onto Miriam's collar bones, severing both arms completely. Miriam's eyes rolled backward into her head as a black deep-colored liquid emanated from both sides of her body. She toppled over and lay at Emily's feet. "As Shawn would say, 'Goodnight Irene!'"

Samuel had exited the building last and with purpose ran quickly toward the barn. He knew who or what was waiting for him. Before he got to within 30 meters of the old dilapidated structure, an unearthly apparition, or specter, exited through the door. It was translucent and showed a deep hideous red in color. Bryant stopped abruptly and faced the ghost-like substance. Samuel then walked slowly toward the barn.

"Hello, Wounded Knee, we finally get a chance to meet face-to-face, if that is what you have above your shoulders. Pay back is about to be rendered, your heathen savage. This is my time now, Indian."

Samuel lunged at the ghost with arms open wide as to drive it backward in a massive bear hug. His arms went through the vapor as if no one was there. Wounded Knee laughed heartily while remaining still. He taunted Samuel, "You didn't hear your wife and daughters scream for mercy, did you, when my Brothers finished our business in the fields that day. Truly pathetic!"

Bryant looked at the Indian specter now five feet away. Samuel abruptly dropped to both knees while looking at Wounded Knee with extreme rage in his eyes. He grabbed two handfuls of dirt in front of him and rose slowly to stand before his adversary. An intense blue light emanated from each of his arms all the way to his fingertips.

"It's time for you to die, Samuel Bryant," the Indian remarked matter-of-factually the savage approached Bryant with confidence and got within two feet of Samuel.

Bryant then thrust out his arms with hands opened wide. What spewed forth was like two lazed beams of blue light that struck the apparition in the chest. Wounded Knee reeled back in surprise against the barn's wall after being struck. In the same instance, his vapor-like appearance changed into true flesh and blood. The blue force propelled him mightily through the door as the hinges came loose releasing shards of old wood everywhere. The 'spirit' lay still until it finally self-combusted into flames just inside where the door once stood.

"I see you finally have 'given up your spirit', your nefarious devil. Rot in Hell!"

Shawn meanwhile came face-to-face with the young black-clad nemesis on the lawn some 15 yards from the back deck of the O'Leary home. They sized one another up without saying a word. Finally, the Evil One broke silence.

"I've been waiting for this for centuries, Shawn. You know that you cannot defeat me, even with the help of your rotund Entity! Today, you have met your match, Boy!"

The ebony staff in the creature's arm reached out and pointed it at Crawford's chest. The streak of reddish fire coming from its tip drove Shawn back several steps. If not for blocking the deathly ray with both palms facing toward the malevolent creature, Crawford would have been incinerated. A look of surprise crossed the face of Shawn's foe. It was all that Crawford needed.

"No one, but me, calls my Boss 'Rotund'!" Shawn said.

Crawford's eyes turned an intense blue. Rays of light were sent forward into the fiery reddish eyes of his opponent. The creature shrieked in pain as he brought both hands to his face. Its body began to smolder at first and then lit up like a bonfire. Soon, not even remnants of ash remained on the ground.

"This is how I repay dirt bags who show disrespect to my Boss." With that, Shawn dropped heavily to both knees in total exhaustion.

The others came over to him quickly. Shawn assured all that he would survive another day and at least one more book written by O'Leary.

The Gray Wolf lay motionless beside the bulkhead. Miriam was now sent to the after-life, as was Wounded Knee. Shawn's adversary was no longer visible anywhere on the lawn's ground. The group wearily went into the O'Leary home.

Inside to the surprise of everyone sat Lynn talking quietly to Sarah, the Nurse who had been lifted out of Shawn's vehicle mere hours ago. Both women were laughing about something and seemed oblivious to what occurred just outside the home.

"Sarah!" Marty shouted. "Are you alright? How did you get here, and, how do you know the O'Leary's?"

"Of course, I'm alright, Marty. I must have dozed off while on duty shortly after 2:15 AM. You know, I woke up in my own bed at home around 2:00 PM yesterday. What was bizarre is that I remembered nothing about what went on at the hospital yesterday. I heard on the news that there was some sort of commotion and that it was reported that a gas line had broken. Somehow, an explosion ensued creating all kinds of problems. The funny thing about it all is that the gas line runs under the ground level to the basement. The explosion was way up on the fourth floor of the hospital. Now, isn't that more than a bit peculiar, Marty?"

The physician looked around the room at everyone and said, "Yes, that is more than strange. However, I'm positive that the local authorities will get to the bottom of it. There has to be some sort of rational explanation, right?"

Sarah replied with a bluish tinge to her eyes that she certainly hoped so.

Shawn looked at Marty and said, "The Boss is always there when you need Him."

In another few hours, the sun would rise on the peaceful community of the Gorham Township.

A wolf howled in the distance.

ABOUT THE AUTHOR

 **TIMOTHY JAMES O'LEARY III** is a retired U.S. Army Lieutenant Colonel with 27 years of active and reserve service for his Country. He served a tour of duty both in Vietnam and the First Persian Gulf War. LTC O'Leary is a Summa Cum Laude Graduate of the Defense Language Institute in Monterey, California where he earned a Diploma in Italian Language Studies. He is also a Graduate of the Army Command and General Staff College located

in Fort Leavenworth, Kansas. Tim served his Country as a Helicopter Pilot and amassed over 2,000 flight hours flying UH-1H and OH-58A aircraft with the United States Army. During Operation Desert Storm, then MAJ O'Leary served as a Medevac Pilot with the 217th Medical Battalion. His final tour of duty was Battalion Commander of the 286th Supply & Service Battalion.

He holds a Bachelor of Arts Degree in Sociology and French, a Masters of Education Degree in Educational Administration and Supervision, as well as the Educational Specialist Degree in the same discipline as the Masters, all from Georgia Southern University. Tim was a Doctoral Candidate in School Administration at the University of Virginia. He also studied Spanish Language for one year at the University of Southern Maine. Tim taught Foreign Language and Social Studies at the Secondary School level in Georgia and was an Assistant Principal at a secondary school in Virginia.

Tim has run 13 marathons to include the Marine Corps in 1984 and the 100th running of the Boston Marathon in 1996. He has been a baseball Umpire for over 40 years and has umpired five Cal Ripken Baseball Series, two in Maryland, and one in Virginia, Louisiana, and Indiana. Tim played Varsity Baseball at Georgia Southern, professional baseball in Italy, and did a baseball tour with the European Continental Cavaliers All-Star Team in South Africa.

Tim and his Wife Lynn reside in Gorham, Maine.